This Toon World book belongs to:

_____

_____

_____

_____

First published in Great Britain by Toon World Ltd 2020
www.toon.world

ISBN: 978-1-8381355-0-8
Printed in England

The website addresses (URLs) included in this book were valid at
the time of going to press. However, it is possible that contents or
addresses may have changed since the publication of this book.
No responsibility for any such changes can be accepted by either
the author or publisher.

For more information contact: info@toon.world

THE CROCODILE WHO COULDN'T SWIM

Written and Illustrated by Lee Attard

A Toon World Book

Codi the Crocodile on a hot summer's day,
Jumped out of bed to go out and play.

He ran down the path
and who did he see?
Who else but Toby the Tiger
'Yippee!'

"Toby my friend,
what shall we play?
Let's play and have fun
on this warm sunny day."

"I'm going to the lake
to cool off and swim,
You're welcome to come
but you'll have to jump in."

Codi then paused
and drooped down his head,
"I simply can't swim"
the little croc said.

Toby felt bad and sad for his friend,
But still carried on to the lake in the end.

Codi felt sad, sad and alone,
He held back his tears on the lonely path home.

Codi looked up and who did he see?
Who else but Hollie the Hippo 'Hee-hee!'

"Hollie my friend,
what shall we play?
Let's play and have fun
on this warm sunny day."

"I'm going to the lake
to splash and have fun,
You can come too
we can float in the sun."

Codi then paused
and timidly said,
"I just can't swim"
and off the croc fled.

Hollie felt bad and sad for her friend,
But still plodded on to the lake in the end.

Codi felt sad, sad and alone,
He held back his tears on the lonely path home.

Nearly back home and who did he see?
Who else but Zoe the Zebra 'Whoopee!'

"Zoe my friend,
what shall we play?
Let's play and have fun
on this warm sunny day."

"I'm going to the lake
to meet Toby and Hollie,
You can come too
we can play some lake volley."

Codi then paused
and quietly uttered,
"But I can't swim"
then off he scuttered.

Zoe felt bad and sad for her friend,
But still trotted on to the lake in the end.

Codi got home and sat on his bed,
Feeling deflated, his hands on his head.

Whilst at the lake his friends couldn't have fun,
Knowing that Codi was home having none.

They thought hard for a while, then Zoe shouted,
"I've got it, get Codi!" and off she scouted.

Before they could ask she was suddenly gone,
They shrugged their shoulders and then hurried on.

Just as Codi had lost all hope,
There was a knock at the door, so he cleared his throat.

"Who is it?" he asked...

"It's us!" they shouted.

"Come with us, quickly!"
his little friends spouted.

Codi shot up from his bed with a smile,
And followed along with his friends for a while.

As they approached the lake, who did they see?
Who else but Zoe the Zebra 'Tee-hee!'

But my oh my, what was she holding?
The mystery solution was clearly unfolding.

"Meet Ducky your new inflatable friend,
Your swimming troubles have come to an end."

Codi was filled with
joy and elation,
He put Ducky on
with no hesitation.

For the first time ever Codi had fun,
Splashing around with his friends in the sun.

Now on a hot summer's day you will see,
Codi and friends, all swimming, carefree.

Pugsy the Pug

Zoe the Zebra

Riley the Reindeer

Geoffrey the Giraffe

Gordon the Goldfish

Ralphie the Rabbit

Miko the Monkey

Codi the Crocodile

Petie the Penguin

Fabia the Flamingo

Ping the Panda

Ollie the Octopus

Henry the Hedgehog

Sonny the Squirrel

Timmy the Tortoise

Susie the Snake

Pauli the Pig

Kimmy the Kitten

Sammy the Snail

Pablo the Parrot

Seth the Sloth

Freeda the Frog

Chachi the Chihuahua

Luca the Lion

Visit the Toon World website for hours of family fun

Meet more lovable animal characters, with new friends being added regularly.

Check out our large selection of FREE printable activities and colouring sheets.

Have endless fun with our ever growing selection of FREE family friendly digital games.

Browse our store of quality merchandise featuring your favourite animal friends.

And lots more fun for you to discover at...
www.toon.world